First published in 2020 by Frances Lincoln Children's Books,
an imprint of The Quarto Group. 400 First Avenue North,
Suite 400, Minneapolis, MN 55401, USA.
T (612) 344-8100 F (612) 344-8692 www.QuartoKnows.com

Original title: Princesse Kevin © 2018 Éditions Glénat,
Couvent Sainte-Cécile - 37, rue Servan - 38000 Grenoble.

ISBN 978-0-7112-5435-0

The illustrations were hand drawn in pen and ink.
Set in Dosis.

Published by Katie Cotton
Translated and edited by Lucy Brownridge
Production by Caragh O'Neill McAleenan

Manufactured in Guangdong, China TT112019
9 8 7 6 5 4 3 2 1

Princess Kevin

WRITTEN BY

Michaël ESCOFFIER

ILLUSTRATED BY

Roland GARRIGUE

Frances Lincoln
Children's Books

Today is costume day at school.
Everyone thinks Kevin will go as
a knight, or a cowboy, or a superhero.

But Kevin is a princess.
People might laugh, but he doesn't care.
Kevin is a princess, and that is that.

He's borrowed a dress, a pair of high heels and
some jewelry from his sister, and some lipstick
from his mom, and now he is a princess. Kevin
knows this costume looks good.

(When you wear a costume, the whole point is that
you become someone totally different. Otherwise,
 it makes no sense to dress up in the first place.)

Anyway, who said that only girls can dress up like princesses?
The girls in his class can dress up as knights and cowboys.
If they can do what they want, so can Kevin.

Speaking of knights, Kevin is quite eager to find one.
A princess without a knight is...just not as cool.
A knight would really complete the look.

The problem is that none of the knights want to hold his hand.

They have this strange idea that boys shouldn't wear pink. It's like they think it's contagious.

And knights are supposed to be brave! These ones are a bunch of chickens.

At least Kevin isn't the only one having a hard time with his costume. Take Chloe. She's supposed to be a dragon, but let's be honest, she looks like a sock.

"No! I am not a sock—I am a dragon!" says Chloe.
Her dad made her costume, but it's clear that he is not very artistic.

"I'm sorry, Chloe. You look really nice, just a little bit
like a sock," says Kevin.
"Thanks, Kevin, you look very nice in that dress."
Kevin blushes and hopes Chloe doesn't notice under
all the makeup.

Kevin is starting to find that looking this good is hard work.
"These high heels are very tricky to walk in. How can
princesses put up with these things? It's torture!"

Kevin's shoes make him wobbly, which makes him get tangled in his dress (which is too long in the first place), which makes him nearly fall over, which makes him grab Chloe's hand.

It is all getting very embarassing.
Maybe this isn't the perfect costume after all.

By the time the show has ended and
the class photo has been taken,

Kevin has had enough
of being a princess.

The problem is, he can't get out of his costume.
"Don't worry, I'll help you. Oh, Kevin, you've got a lot to learn before you can be a real princess," giggles Chloe.
"You must be joking! I don't want to be a real princess. It's way too complicated. Next year, I'm keeping it simple," Kevin says.

"I'm going to be

a mermaid!"